R2-D2 and C-3PO were in trouble.
The droids had escaped
from the evil Darth Vader.
But they were lost on a hot
and sandy planet.

R2-D2 was short and white.
C-3PO was tall and gold.
C-3PO wanted to stop walking.
But R2-D2 wanted to keep going.
He was on a secret mission.

STAR WARS™

TROUBLE ON TATOOINE

WRITTEN BY NATE MILLICI

ART BY PILOT STUDIO

DISNEY

LUCASFILM PRESS

Los Angeles • New York

All rights reserved. Published by Disney • Lucasfilm Press, an imprint of Disney Book Group. No part of this book may be reproduced or transmitted in any form or by any means, electronic or mechanical, including photocopying, recording, or by any information storage and retrieval system, without written permission from the publisher. For information address Disney • Lucasfilm Press, 1101 Flower Street, Glendale, California 91201.

Printed in the United States of America

First Edition, May 2017   10 9 8 7 6 5 4 3 2 1

Library of Congress Control Number on file

FAC-029261-17076

ISBN 978-1-4847-9934-5

Visit the official *Star Wars* website at: www.starwars.com.

SUSTAINABLE
FORESTRY
INITIATIVE

Certified Sourcing

www.sfiprogram.org
SFI-01415

R2-D2 rolled on without C-3PO.
He needed to finish his mission.
It started to get dark.
R2-D2 started to get nervous.

Then a small creature jumped out
and stunned R2-D2!
It was a Jawa.
The Jawas carried R2-D2
back to their sandcrawler.

Strange droids filled
the sandcrawler.
R2-D2 was scared.
Then R2-D2 heard a voice. . . .

It was C-3PO!
The Jawas had taken C-3PO, too.
R2-D2 and C-3PO were glad
they had found each other!

But then the sandcrawler
rolled to a stop.
R2-D2 and C-3PO
were going to be sold!

R2-D2 and C-3PO lined up with
the other droids.
They were in front of a farm.
The farm belonged to Uncle Owen,
Aunt Beru, and Luke Skywalker.

Uncle Owen needed droids
to help him on the farm.
Uncle Owen picked C-3PO
and a red-and-white droid.
R2-D2 was sad.

But smoke started to pour
from the red-and-white droid.
C-3PO told Luke Skywalker
to pick R2-D2 instead.
R2-D2 happily rolled
toward the farm.

It was Luke's job
to clean the droids.
When Luke cleaned R2-D2,
a hologram appeared!

The hologram was of
a girl in a white dress.
The girl was asking for help.
The girl's message was for a man
named Obi-Wan Kenobi.
This was R2-D2's secret mission!

Luke told his aunt and uncle
about R2-D2's message.
Could it be for Old Ben Kenobi?
Old Ben lived across the desert.
Uncle Owen told Luke to forget
about R2-D2's message.

But Luke longed for an adventure.
Little did Luke know
he was about to go on one!

R2-D2 had left the farm
to find Old Ben!

But it was too late for Luke
to go after the little droid.

The next morning, Luke and C-3PO
raced across the desert to find R2-D2.

Luke and C-3PO found R2-D2.
But they also found something else. . . .

Sand People!
Sand People were mean creatures
that lived in the desert.
They attacked Luke!

But a man in long brown robes
scared off the Sand People.

It was Old Ben!
Luke asked if Old Ben knew
a man named Obi-Wan Kenobi.
Old Ben told Luke that
he was Obi-Wan Kenobi!
Old Ben took Luke back to his hut.

Old Ben was once a Jedi Knight.
Jedi Knights protected
the galaxy from evil.
Ben had known Luke's father.
Luke's father had
been a Jedi Knight, too!

Old Ben said he had a gift for Luke.
It had belonged to Luke's father.

It was Luke's father's lightsaber!
Jedi Knights used lightsabers and
the Force to help the galaxy.
The Force gave the Jedi their power.
The Force was an energy field
created by all living things.

R2-D2 beeped.
He *still* hadn't finished
his mission!

Finally, R2-D2 showed
the hologram to Ben.
Ben asked Luke to help him.

Ben wanted to train Luke to become
a Jedi Knight like Luke's father.

Luke agreed to help
R2-D2 and Old Ben.
His next adventure was about to begin!